Marduk

Marduk

DAVE BRAY
and
THOMAS FULGHUM

Resource *Publications*

An imprint of *Wipf and Stock Publishers*
199 West 8th Avenue • Eugene OR 97401

MARDUK

ISBN 13: 978-1-55635-092-4

Illustrated by Robert C. Seibert
Cover illustration by Jason Lewis

We would like to dedicate this book to the Lord Jesus Christ and we pray that He will use it to His glory and honor.
We would also like to thank our parents who always encouraged our imaginations, and who reared us in the love and knowledge of Jesus.
Also, we would like to thank those who prayed for us in the writing of this book. And thank you for reading our book; we had a lot of fun writing it.

Contents

Prologue

Some may dismiss the story that I'm about to unfold as a mere childish fantasy, but it is based upon hard reality. I know this because much of it revolves around my own life. My name is Victor Steinhouse, and I affirm that this story is true, but the reader must decide what is truth and what is fiction.

The time is Earth year 2333; a year forever remembered by many as the beginning of a horrible new reality for civilization. Fortunately, the year is long buried in the past.

The location is the city of Chicago, in the state of Illinois. This was one of the last remaining cities in the United States, because of the great destruction of that era.

* * *

When it started, all the United States was having inter-city wars. The Legionnaire had ordered that a huge monument of himself be constructed, first of all in Washington D.C., and then he ordered that one be constructed in every state capitol of the whole country. Not only did he want a different monument in each city, he also did not want any duplicates in style or shape. Soon the cities were getting quite involved in their planning and building of the monuments, comparing one to another, boasting that theirs was classier.

The conflict and tension between the cities grew more and more competitive, fierce, and then violent. As the years went by, the forms of attack became more and more advanced and destructive.

At first, because of the possible side effects, inter-city war was not even considered. Then, one city began by attacking another city. The attack was aimed at defacing or marring the other city's monuments. That city would, in turn, attempt retaliation. Each man fought for his own city. Tempers flared and revenge was the desired motivation.

The final straw that broke the camel's back was when the first monument, which the Legionnaire had constructed in Washington D.C., had profanity sprayed all over it with a paint laced with nitroglycerine. The next day when the sun came out and heated up the profanity, it started glowing; within minutes it exploded, demolishing the monument and damaging the buildings around it.

When the Legionnaire heard of this, in rage he declared war against New York City, which had instigated the vandalism, even going so far as to use the Liquid Death Missile, a weapon designed to have the same explosive properties as the ancient twentieth century nuclear weapons, plus what seems to be hundreds of times its power and capabilities, causing massive destruction. The outer shell is made from a metal named micazirconakite, a compound metal made up of mica and various crushed zirconium gem stones melted together, capable of being molded or shaped into almost any form.

Because of its high mica content, it is very light in weight and is silver-gray in color. As a result of the zirconium, it glitters brilliantly and is very strong. Some micazirconakite, when in liquid form and mixed with a secret explosive chemical, causes an extremely dangerous chain reaction if fired in an air-tight container from high altitudes. When fired, the two chemicals mix and the results explain the name of the Liquid Death Missile.

Soon, other cities followed the example of the Legionnaire and fought with various weapons that were equally as destructive. Before long, all the cities had come under heavy attack. Most of the major cities were destroyed in less than a month.

Only Chicago, Phoenix, and Denver survived this bloody stain on U.S. history. Because he had been on a business trip to Chicago when Washington D.C. was demolished, the Legionnaire's life was spared.

The war started because of mans' pride as each of the cities set out to prove that it was the best. "I am better than the rest!" "My monument is more original, beautiful, or unique!" "My defense or attack mode is more effective!"

The men built massive monuments to prove their superiority, and soon were worshipping the monuments themselves as superior beings, believing that they had supernatural powers.

There were many stories that they believe give credence to their worship of their structures. The first story goes like this: A man lost his family in a huge crowd of people. After spending many hours looking for them, he almost gave up. In his desperation, he yelled up to one of the monuments, pleading that it show him where his family was.

Supposedly, or so he claimed, the monument responded by casting its shadow on him and in a long straight path on the ground. He followed the shadow, which led the man right to his family.

The second story took place once when there were fierce thunderstorms throughout Chicagoland. It rained for two days solid without letting up and there was flooding everywhere. Fierce lightning struck all the buildings in Chicago, except for the Chicago Monument, and the inhabitants of Chicago considered this a proof of the Monument's preeminence. It's no wonder that the people confused circumstances involving the buildings with supposed proof of their superiority.

And many men, women, and children worshipped the Monuments. Each sunrise, the bodies of people who thought differently than those in authority would be sacrificed; those considered a threat to their power; those that they felt lessened their power, which included the elderly, the disabled, and the Followers, (the title given to those of us who followed Jesus and his teachings). I am proud to be a Follower who survived this holocaust.

Emotions raged as the destructive conflict continued. Childlike temper-tantrums were exploding, just as the various array of bombs were blowing up parts of the United States, leaving behind a cratered, pitted landscape, millions of casualties and demolished cities. Men were like a bunch of hungry locusts, destroying everything in their way.

The authorities had replaced God's law with three basic rules:

1) The ultimate authority is the Legionnaire, and then, the Black Widows.

2) Each individual is required to work where the authorities indicate, without discussion.

3) Anyone whose lack of strength or intelligence would weaken progress must die.

Many people instructed their children to follow these rules. They were so brainwashed by the Legionnaire's propaganda that they did not know what they were doing. With each Monument's construction, the authorities became mightier than before. I can remember seeing buildings much taller than I thought humanly possible, and of the most unexpected shapes and colors.

* * *

At this time, some of us Followers were working jobs in the
vissionelles (or churches, as old-timers used to call them).
We knew that such jobs were illegal, but we would rather
serve God than sinful man. We knew that God would deliver us from this dark time in which we were living.

And God always gave us encouragement when we
needed it the most. Faithful and True; that's who He is,
and He, from the beginning of time, has been gathering a

people for Himself. He stands behind His children, never leaving or abandoning us.

Several of us boldly spoke up against the sin of idolatry, which was so prevalent. Some people would listen to what we said and become believers like us, but sadly, many Followers were killed for their faith.

These martyrs were like newly hatched butterflies: on earth, they were caterpillars, simply crawling the ground. Then they were in heaven with Jesus, free from the sin that so easily entangles all of us.

Other Followers kept their faith hidden; they were fearful of their oppressors, of the results of being discovered. In fear they would give up their faith, and in place of a relationship with the True God, they would join the rest of man's evil society and worship a lie.

But as the Monuments got bigger and bigger, so did the destructive attacks on the remaining cities. In the end, Chicago blew up both Phoenix and Denver, and stood alone. With that came more unmentionable terror for the Followers. There were some people, who had once professed to believe in Christianity, who spied on and reported fellow Followers to the authorities.

The result of the capture of these believers was usually fatal. One of the terrible ways the Followers were persecuted was that some of them were sent to Marduk's lab. There the Followers were experimented on like guinea pigs, being used for the testing of the effects of various new kinds of corrosive chemicals.

Marduk was an extreme individual, for an extremely dark time in U. S. history. Even his name, Marduk, was the name of a Babylonian demon god. Being a military technical genius, he was employed by the Black Widows to make weapons that were more destructive than the Liquid Death Missile itself, for implementation in the wars.

He had an extremely big ego, and seemed to derive pleasure from inflicting pain on others. He was ruthless; the taking of lives did not seem to faze him at all and seemed to harden his heart even more. Marduk had been abandoned and abused as a child and had learned to fend for himself, caring about nobody else.

The Black Widows were merchants of death, with a venomous bite. They were the leaders of the group that worshipped the Monuments, and were opposed to the worship of any other object or god. They were adamantly opposed to the Followers.

They were tall and lanky, and were clad from head to toe in black. They were like spiders, lurking in the darkness, spying on the people. A hovercraft was their mode of transportation, and they would zip along above the surface of the ground, never touching it. Their bodies were covered with various types of advanced technical weaponry, and at their fingertips was sudden death for their victims. They were looking for anyone who believed other than how they did, and when they caught someone, the punishment was usually fatal, at best.

The Black Widows kept their eyes out for the Followers, looking for grounds on which they could accuse us. They prided themselves on being fair and never arresting anybody without first having proof of their guilt.

The Followers, in obedience to Jesus Christ whom they followed, went out in groups of two or three to share the truth about Jesus with the people of Chicago, and offer them a share of the freedom that He had bestowed on them. They emphatically told the people that they had to accept Jesus as their Lord and Savior and He would forgive their sin and they would be free for eternity.

So it was inevitable that a confrontation would take place.

I

Graduation

GRADUATION! THIS was the culmination of many years of hard work on the part of Paul and his classmates. Today, all over the county, families would be uniting together, rejoicing in the accomplishment of their peers and family members. It was a time for celebration; a time for remembrance; a time for musicians to play songs that triggered memories; a time for smiles and a time for tears.

It was the year 2322, and many folks were gathered at the John Hancock Space Observatory Recreational Center, in Chicago, Illinois. for a long awaited graduation ceremony. Paul had been a student for eight years at the Chicago Space System where he studied elaborate architecture, and the creation of bionic cybernetic body parts.

The Chicago Space System was rather small in size, but it produced the sharpest minds in the entire world. The Recreational Center was a gold-leafed dome-shaped structure, with Amethyst crystal windows.

The students were taught the basics by instructional robots, which had vast resources of information. They were five feet tall, with cherry-red glowing eyes, metal bodies, and computer-generated human voices.

Classes were held Monday through Friday, from 6:00 am to 7:00 pm, with testing sometimes on Saturdays. Attention in class was crucial, and tardiness was not accepted. So graduation was a big accomplishment for anyone, and an overwhelming one for Paul, who was intellectually challenged.

In the audience that day, proudly watching as their son crossed the podium to receive his diploma, were Peter and Martha Steinhouse. The wrinkles on their faces symbolized the wisdom that they had acquired over the years. Their blue eyes sparkled like diamonds, and showed warmth and compassion, as well as the pride that they felt for their son.

They smiled, remembering all the tears and work that it had required to bring him to this point. They remembered that when Paul was a child in Youngin' School there had been times when, because of his learning difficulties, they had wondered if he would ever complete Mind-Shaping Academy.

Now, as he was graduating from techniversity, they praised the Lord for His strength and for the promise that Paul had claimed throughout the whole trying experience: "I can do all things through Christ who enables me."

After everyone had received their graduation certificates, suddenly all the graduates, clad in their purple gowns and triangular caps with gold leaf trim, threw their caps into the air and cheered enthusiastically. The graduates were excited by the fact that they had finally earned their degrees; they were also thrilled that early tomorrow they would be boarding a spacecraft and together they would go to the Platoon System in the bordering galaxy for a week.

The Platoon System was a recreational masterpiece that had been constructed during the year 2318. In it were different planets—one for music and dance, one for sports, one for movies, and one with beaches for swimming and water skiing and, of course, tanning. This senior trip was the trip of a lifetime. The graduates would be able to spend time on all or any one of the planets that they wished.

Paul graduated with his childhood sweetheart, Esther Crimpet. They had been in love long before they could remember. What better time, they asked each other, to be married than while you are on Sunset Beach in "Loveland?" So that is what they both chose.

Not thinking about what their parents would have to say about it, the two of them made their decision and were married on July 10, by one of the Followers who was a pastor that resided on the planet. This was only three days after their excursion had begun. The service was held at 11:00 a.m., in the "Building of Light" on "Twilight Rock."

The visionelle itself was a work of beauty; its walls and ceiling were made of various clear and transparent gemstones like quartz crystal, highlighted by topaz, zirconium, and aquamarine. The floors were tiled with turquoise and amethyst, and the pews were made of glass. The sun's rays shone through the steeply slanted roof, sending hundreds of various colored reflections sparkling throughout the northexodium, dancing in rhythmic harmony. The whole visionelle glittered like the waters of the sea and gave the sensation of being in a mystic fairyland.

The sweethearts did not relish the thought of being married apart from their parents, but neither did they desire to pass up such a wonderful opportunity to be married in this celestial sanctuary, so they recorded it all on holographic disk, to be seen later by their families upon their arrival back on earth.

When Paul and Esther arrived home they shared with their parents that they had indeed been married while on their senior excursion. They were almost surprised to receive joyful congratulations as both pairs of parents had been hoping that this would happen for a very long time.

They were thankful to the Lord that their children had found another Follower of such a good quality with whom to be united. They invited all of their friends over for a party to celebrate the new marriage.

Everyone watched the holographic disk as it was projected on the broad screen. Friends and family members who could cook prepared delicacies to be eaten at the occasion. The camaraderie and unity of the Followers was enriching.

Situations such as this one were happy memories in a darkening world. Life was becoming more and more difficult for the Followers. With each passing day, or so it seemed, new edicts were passed by the iron-fist Legionnaire that either contradicted our beliefs, or hampered our worship.

As time progressed, the situation for the Followers got tougher and tougher. This was true not only for the parents, the adults, but also for the children and teens. The teachers became more and more restricting; at first the young Followers were told that praying to any being other than the Legionnaire, by means of the monuments, was forbidden; the results of doing so could be very serious.

If ever a Follower was caught reading God's Word, the punishment was a public flogging, and the Bible was burnt. For the most part, the Holy Scriptures became something that one had to hide to read, which seemed so very much against what God had planned when He gave us His Word. "Your Word is a Lamp for my feet and a Light for my path." (Psalm 119:105)

The Followers of Jesus Christ were then no longer permitted entrance into public places such as shopping centers, restaurants, or even educational facilities. The majority found the Followers to be extremely obtrusive and offensive to their daily way of life.

More governmental officials took bribes, and perverted justice. Assassination of public officials became as commonplace as summer sunshine. The love of most grew stone cold. In the Chicago as a whole, one women was raped every ten seconds, and then the women started raping men. Men and women alike were conceited and proud, not caring about anybody but themselves.

When the situation had gotten worse, the Steinhouses and most of the rest of the Followers who were members of their flock moved into Chicago, and lived in underground caverns.

These dark, murky tunnels that permeated the city had been installed when the Legionnaire, newly in office, had constructed a totally redesigned road system.

Life in the tunnels was not easy; it was smelly, dirty, and slimy when it rained, but the fact that the Followers were safe and able to live together was all that mattered. Whenever they got depressed over their living situation, they simply closed their eyes, and imagined the streets of gold where they'd soon be walking with Jesus. Sometimes they joked about being like the early Church in the Catacombs.

In six months, Esther became pregnant, and nine months later she and Paul became the proud parents of twin boys. They named my brother "Stephen", because in the New Testament, Stephen had been such a good example of suffering triumphantly for the Lord. They named me "Victor," because that is just what we are in Christ.

Although we were twins, we were definitely not clones. Stephen was very much like Dad, who was a builder; Dad was a creative genius, and was extremely gifted at visualizing things even before they had yet been built. He was the one who wrote up the design for the pools of Venus; the Jupiter Super, a home for the elderly, was also his design. Dad even used some of Stephen's ideas for the additions to his buildings.

At home, Stephen was always coming up with new, helpful inventions for doing things around the house. He was nicknamed "Braino" for his intelligence and scientific creativity.

I, on the other hand, was very much like my mother. She taught me various art forms, and we spent a great deal of time studying and creating art and music together. She helped me learn to paint and to draw. She also taught me spelling and grammar. I credit her for teaching me to use my God-given abilities for the glory of the Lord. I taught myself how to write stories and dialogues for plays.

During our time together, I learned how much she depended on prayer. She taught me to "pray without ceasing," to include God my Heavenly Father in everything. I think that what I learned about prayer from my Mom is what brought me through the oncoming years without an emotional breakdown.

On one occasion, when we were going through a horribly difficult experience, my Mom came up quietly from behind me, and in her quiet, gentle way, began praying:

"The Lord is my Shepherd; I shall lack nothing."

"Do you know what that means, Victor?" she asked me. I shook my head, and so she continued. "The shepherd loved and cared for the sheep; he provided for the sheep, fed the sheep, comforted the sheep, and protected the sheep. When a lion or bear attacked, the shepherd interceded, risking his own life to protect those in his care. As you and I just quoted, the Lord is my Shepherd. Jesus Himself has promised to do all of these things for us, his sheep.

"Sheep cannot protect themselves. They are stupid animals, and are quite helpless. In His Word, sheep are exactly the animal that God, being all-knowing, chose to compare us to. We, too, need the hand of a kind, loving Master to reach in and direct and guide us. We need His protection and provision and love.

"Let's continue. 'The Lord is my Shepherd; I shall lack nothing. He makes me lie down in green pastures, He leads me beside quiet waters, He restores my soul.'

"Victor, though the situation right now does not seem like "green pastures" or "quiet waters," or anything peaceful, for that matter, God wants to offer us perfect peace in our hearts and minds. God promises that peace to His children when He says, "I will keep him at perfect peace whose mind is stayed on Me, because he trusts in Me."

"Continuing, 'He guides me in paths of righteousness for His Name's sake.'

"Our not following the evil rulers around us, and our being willing to suffer like this for Him brings Him glory; it does the same when we respond in obedience to Him, because God's ways are righteous."

"'Even though I walk through the valley of the shadow of death,' like we are presently doing, Vic, 'I will fear no evil, for You are with me.' Praise God, He never leaves us! Never!

"'Your rod and your staff, they comfort me.'" Victor, a shepherd uses the rod and the staff for different things. Sometimes, he must gently prod or poke or hit with his staff a sheep that is going off in a dangerous direction. God sometimes has to allow for us to go through difficulties, but we have the promise from scripture that 'in all things God works for the good of those who love Him, who have been called according to His purpose.'" (Rom. 8:28 NIV)

"At times, the shepherd uses His rod to ward off something or someone who is attacking or endangering his sheep. God promises to do the same with us. That is a big promise, Vic, and we can be assured that everything that we suffer has a way in which it will result for our good, and God's benefit. Isn't it great to know that everything difficult results in something beneficial?

"'You prepare a table before me in the presence of my enemies.' When we are in a conflict, God gives us peace; even when in the sight of our enemies, we can sit down for a meal with Him.

"'You anoint my head with oil'; is a sign of dedication.

"'My cup overflows' is a sign of blessing."

"'Surely goodness and love will follow me all the days of my life, and I will dwell in the house of the Lord forever.' Victor, God is good, and He is Love Personified; He loved us so much He sent His Son Jesus to die in our place. He will never leave us, all the days of our lives. For those of us who have accepted Christ to be our Savior and Lord, when our time here on earth comes to an end, we will go to live in His house forever!"

"How can I accept Him, Mom?"

"If you believe in your heart that Jesus was God's Son, and that He came to earth to die for your sins, in your place, simply talk to Him and tell Him that you want to accept His gift, and become a member of His family. Ask Him to forgive your sins, and to come into your heart, to help you to obey Him."

Right there and then I made my decision.

* * *

Stephen and I went to "Youngin' School" together. In the middle of my seventh grade term Mom gave birth to our sister, Ruth. She was a nice addition to our family, and we both enjoyed having a little sister. When she was only five years old, we could see that there were many of the attributes of both Mom and Dad showing up in her. The next two years went by quickly. Stephen and I both wanted to go to "Mind-Shaping Academy," but this was out of the question.

The role of Legionnaire had changed drastically, or so my parents told us. In our history class, we learned that when America began, the Legionnaire, or at that time, called "president," ruled for and was held accountable to the people. Now, the Legionnaire was held accountable to nobody, and ruled with an iron fist.

Not only were the "Mind-Shaping Academies" and "Techniversities" shutting down, but the Legionnaire also issued the decree that the disabled and "religiously in-clined," which of course included the Followers, could not have public education. There were rumors of wars, but in reality no one really knew what was happening.

2

The Menacing Legionnaire

T HE MENACING Legionnaire's Empire became more and more corrupt, and "every intent of the thoughts of his heart was only evil continually." (Genesis 6:5) The Legionnaire himself was a grotesque sight; he was 4 feet, eight inches tall, and his eyes glared at you in such a way that it made you feel naked. His breath had the disgusting smell of rotting teeth. His favorite food was live fish, sprinkled with mustard.

The Legionnaire was a cruel man, and when he looked at his subjects, he did not see them as human beings, or as individuals, but rather as challenges, problems that needed to be resolved.

The Legionnaire and his wife had a huge disagreement and she has never been seen since. However, his housekeeper was once heard exclaiming about the many bags of fresh-ground meat that he had accumulated in the freezer overnight.

The Legionnaire's housekeeper/cook did her very best to keep her employer happy. She always dressed neatly in her pressed uniform, and tried to be sure that everything was in tip-top condition. As she was making out her meal plans, she went to check on the freezer, to see what cuts of meat she had available. She opened one bag to check on it, and let out a hideous scream. When she had peaked in the bag, she had seen three mutilated fingers. As she lurched, she dropped the bag. As it fell to the floor, a human eyeball rolled out at her feet.

When the Legionnaire heard her screams, he came running into the room to see what the problem was. When he saw the cook and her reaction to what she had found, he became belligerent. Walking over to the frightened house-keeper, with a snarl on his face he scoffed, "This is nothing!" With that, he scooped up the eyeball off the floor, went over to the sink and rinsed the dust off it in running water, popped it into his mouth, and left, chewing emphatically. The housekeeper fainted dead away.

Another example of the Legionnaire's inhumane tactics was that prayer to anything or anyone other than the Monuments was made illegal, with the threat of death to anyone caught praying to any other God.

The Legionnaire was told that some of the biggest breakers of that law were the children and this upset him. "We must train them, and get complete obedience from them while they are still young, or they'll learn to disobey and think that they can get away with it when they are older. We must clamp down on them."

The Legionnaire continued with his evil plotting. "We must think of a punishment that is very visible and horrifying; one that will make the students want to conform to our demands in the future."

With that, he instructed the teachers to inform him if ever a child was caught praying. It was not long before such an incident occurred. Not knowing what the punishment was going to be, a teacher informed the Legionnaire of a group of students who were caught praying before their meal at her school.

In his anger, the Legionnaire instructed the Black Widows, his band of evilness, to string them up in the center of the playground, in view of all the other students. "Then get some mad, rabid, hungry pit-bulls, and set them free in the playground. Force all the students to stand there and watch their friends being consumed by the dogs. This will make each one of them think twice before disobeying me."

Even as the Legionnaire's orders were being carried out, the children being slaughtered were heard by everyone to be praying for strength, and then even praising Jesus as they were swept into His presence.

The rest of the students will never forget that scene! Most of them, in fact, we all had nightmares for months, even years. The one thing that gave power to the recollection, and even caused some of the children to accept Christ for themselves, was the memory of the look of peace and even joy on the faces of the kids as they stepped from life on earth into life eternal.

On another occasion, a group of Followers were celebrating the birthday of one of the children. A rather large group of them had gathered together. They were playing games and having fun. A next-door neighbor who was not a Follower and had no respect for "those rebellious breakers of the law," called the Legionnaire, and informed him.

It seems that when the group started singing praise songs, this neighbor become very worked up. "There is a group of the Followers in the house next door; they are being very vocal about their praise of a God other than the Monuments."

At that, the Legionnaire yelled back, "How dare they so openly disobey my orders!" He then called for the Black Widows, who ran out to their Hovercrafts, and zipped away in search of the Followers.

When they arrived, things were just as the informant had said, so the Black Widows circled the house, and torched it. The Followers could be heard continuing with their praise songs to God in Heaven, but the volume became less and less, as one-by-one, they passed into His presence.

And finally, many of the Followers were going one by one into a nearby forest. The Black Widows grew suspicious of them, because they were all heading in the same direction, though via different routes. The Black Widows secretly followed one group, and saw that deep in the forest, all the Followers were entering a cave for one of their forbidden religious gatherings.

Soon the Black Widows heard some notes being played on a harmonica, and then all the Followers were singing as well. As they sang, the Black Widows could tell that they were doing more than simply producing notes, but that they were communicating or singing to something or someone. The song they sang, ironically, was about standing firm when troubles come.

> "When the World is against us
> And the troubles and hard times come,
> Thank you Lord for being with us
> Your love is enough for anyone.
> Jehovah Jireh, my Provider,
> You're the strength I need for every day,
> Holy Spirit, Indwelling fire,
> You complete me in every way."

The Black Widows took this as a challenge. "Well, men, let's see if we can get them to recant!"

The merchants of death hid in the bushes, watching as more and more people entered the cave. When they saw that no more people were coming, they stormed into the cave. There they found the Followers having a worship service. So they killed the children in front of the parents, and then slaughtered the adults, as well.

My parents and my sister were three of the Followers who were massacred that day. I did not know what had happened to my brother. He just simply disappeared without a trace. Somehow, I escaped, but I had nightmares for weeks after the incident.

I could have been chained by bitterness and hatred for the rest of my life, but God in his awesome love delivered me from that, and in its place ultimately gave me a sense of forgiveness and concern for the Black Widows.

But for the first two years after that incident my life was a series of bad dreams and fear. I would slink from shadow to shadow, fearing the Black Widows, always afraid that they were right behind me.

It was during one of those times when I was so very afraid of being found that I remembered where my parents had told me that they found their help. Dad had said that whenever he was afraid, he would turn in his Bible to Psalm 139.

So I rummaged through my hip pocket and pulled out Dad's small New Testament with Psalms and Proverbs. I turned quickly to Psalm 139, and read; ". . . You notice everything I do, and everywhere I go . . . And with Your powerful arm you protect me from every side . . ." This renewed my faith in God, and revived my desire to share Him with others. I no longer remained afraid in the shadows, but God gave me boldness to come out into the light. There I met other believers who also were desirous of sharing their faith. They invited me to move into their community and share their food and enjoy their fellowship. I did and each day we seemed we grew closer to each other and closer to the God we loved and served.

Daily the community grew as new people made commitments to follow Christ. We knew that it was not foolproof, as any day someone could make a profession to follow Christ and be accepted into the community only to betray us. We simply prayed that Christ would protect us from the evil one, and that he would direct our paths. More than just to live a problem-free life we wanted to be used by God to make Him proud of us.

That was when we met Irgo, a man who had grown up in Dallas, Texas. He seemed to fall in so well with all our young people. The mothers trusted him with babysitting their children. I even thought that He and I became good friends. He seemed so sincere, desiring to grow in the Lord.

However, the Black Widows had approached him secretly and offered him an exorbitant amount of money if he would betray us and tell them where our hideout was. I'm not sure what made him think that they would keep their promise and pay him anything, but he met with them and told them all about where we lived. As far as I know, as soon as they had the information, they did away with him. We never saw him again.

The day before we were captured had been very productive. Many people heard the good news and believed. We were elated with the response that we had gotten and were very encouraged at how God was blessing our efforts. It was great how God knows the end from the beginning. He knew that we would need the encouragement for the oncoming experience.

When we arrived at home that afternoon we were surprised to find the entrance to the hideout open and unconcealed. As we approached, Black Widows on their hovercrafts suddenly came zipping toward us from every direction. They hit each of us over the head with a stunning blow that knocked us out cold.

When we regained consciousness we found that we were in a dark chamber that smelled rancid. I recognized some of the other prisoners; they were Followers who had been previously captured, whom the Black Widows had taken to their experimentation lab.

We knew that Marduk worked in a secret room, attached adjacent to the main lab. No one but Marduk himself knew how to get into the secret room, as the entrance was well concealed.

The lab was hideous, and the utensils, ingredients, and tabletops were filthy. His metal desk had three drawers which were crammed with papers, pencils, pens, rubber bands, file folders, paper bags, a half-eaten apple, and a dinner from last week; his chair was on its side to the left of an overflowing garbage can. On one wall was a huge mirror, cracked from corner to corner.

We believers were ready to face the mad scientist with courage, but we did have some resentment and apprehension about the harsh experimentation that was being performed on us. We grieved the loss of our loved ones as they were being blown up or eaten away by corrosive acid, or had vital organs and/ or other body parts extracted.

The only thing that brought us through the experience so triumphantly was the fact that we knew that Christ would never leave or forsake us, and His Holy Spirit, living within us, constantly gave us courage and hope. The fact that Christ died on the cross for us, made us feel privileged and joyful to be able to die for Him.

I recalled hearing in visionelle when I was a child, that, "The blood of the martyrs is the seed of the church." It was comforting for me to know that the future Followers of my Lord Jesus Christ would grow and become stronger because of the difficult experiences my friends and I were presently having.

3

Remorse and Repentance

IT WAS one of those dark, rainy nights in Chicago, and
Marduk was deep in the cave, at his chemical lab. He
pushed a hidden button on the mirror that covered the
major part of one of the walls, and the secret entrance to

the lab in which he did the experiments on the Followers opened.

To most people who came into the lab, there was simply a large mirror on the wall, but as Marduk pushed the button, the door on which the mirror was hung slid open, revealing the blood; the chemicals, the jars with floating body parts taken from innocent martyrs, and above all, the unseen, yet very easily imagined pain. The room was eerie and dark, and reeked from the stench of rotting flesh, and was ice cold.

Marduk entered the room and walked to the corner where there was a narrow door. The rusty hinges squeaked as he opened the door and he was hit with the overwhelming odor of vomit mixed with urine, which perfumed the air.

Walking down the narrow hallway, holding his nose, he approached a cell that was inhabited by twelve people, and called for three of us by name to come forth. "Victor Steinhouse, Dr. Roberts, Dr. Malerie, you will come with me to the main chemical experimentation lab."

My friends gasped and each squeezed my hand as I walked somberly to the door.

"The nine of us will be praying for you," one whispered. As Dr. Roberts, the oldest man in the group, stood up, a tear rolled down his wife's wrinkled face. "Remember that God will never leave you nor forsake you," she said. Dr. Malerie handed her nursing baby girl to her husband. After kissing her on the head, she whispered, "I love you" in her ear. Her thoughts jumped back to her growing-up years, in Idaho. She remembered that the last thing she had heard from her Mother before the bombing had taken her life had been just that, "I love you."

Marduk then shackled our wrists with dirty, old handcuffs, and began walking us briskly back up the darkened corridor. When, at last, we reached the lab, Marduk had us, one by one, lay down on a table where he secured us, preventing our escape. He then walked over to the shelves where he stored his chemicals, and began mixing up a dangerously strong concoction.

But something went wrong, terribly wrong, something that would change Marduk's life forever. As he was in the midst of mixing some powerful chemicals, the room suddenly began to shake wildly, and Marduk realized that an earthquake was hitting. Before he could move away, the shock threw the bottles of volatile chemicals crashing to the floor, and the contents began to mix with each other.

Marduk froze with terror; he saw that some of the chemicals had begun to form a dangerous gas. And then, with no further warning, there was a tremendous explosion. Marduk tried to shield himself with his hands from the flying glass and chemicals, but it was too late for that. His body was covered with a flesh-eating acid.

As Marduk screamed in agony, the second shock wave hit and threw him violently to the floor. Simultaneously, almost all the glass in the lab blew up into tiny slivers, many of which headed in his direction. Marduk screamed in agony as hundreds of glass shards penetrated his flesh.

It was as if a multitude of tiny knives were stabbing him all at once. The same slivers, directed by God, simply cut our bonds. Marduk screamed in agony and instead of running away, we concerned Followers ran to his aid. Before he became unconscious, he could feel his body burning; burning like paper in a fireplace. His skin got sandpaper dry and then broke open; blistering pus that was cold and rather slimy began trickling down his body. Parts of his skin began stretching and becoming hideously disfigured.

His body started to shrink. One of his legs dissolved completely, leaving behind a bloody stump. His finger and toe-nails were growing rapidly and his hair caught fire and was singed off in a matter of seconds. His skin turned the color of puke-green. He let out a howl of agony, and then faded away into a restless unconsciousness.

As I mentioned, there were nine Followers left in the cell, waiting to be used as guinea pigs. The moment that the shock waves had begun, their chains began to tremble violently. One by one, the clamps broke and the chains fell to the floor. During the second shock wave, the gates began to vibrate, and the hinges broke. When the third shock wave had passed, the prisoners found that there was nothing holding them in their bonds. "Hey!" exclaimed Silvester, Dr. Malerie's husband. "This is just like in Paul's day. Remember when God rescued Paul and Silas from the prison? Our God sure is faithful!"

Mrs. Roberts then yelled, "Let's go check on the others! I wonder how God rescued them!"

Four hours later, when Marduk woke up, he was on the ground, on his back in a big pool of his own blood. He looked all around the now destroyed lab, and noticed that the very people that he had planned to use for his experiments surrounded him. He thought this was strange, because he had expected that we would have all died from the shock waves, because of our weakened condition.

Marduk's paranoid mind made him fearful that we were going to do experiments on him, as he had been doing on us. Instead, though, he saw a spark of love and compassion in our eyes. We were a rather filthy bunch of people, covered with plaster dust, but without a scratch on our bodies. We noticed how Marduk looked, too; he knew this because he heard us whispering to each other and could sense that we were trying not to stare at him. He had an intense, throbbing headache and felt a deep burning sensation all over his body. It wasn't until he went to rub the sweat off his brow that he realized that his whole body was penetrated with narrow splinters of glass.

Marduk muttered to himself, "I've had enough of this!" He tried to get up, but Dr. Roberts spoke up and instructed him, "It would be better for you if you would get some rest. You've been through quite an ordeal. Today we will try to figure out what to do with the fragments of glass."

Marduk then muttered, "Why should I accept help from the scum that I've been experimenting on?! Why should I trust you, of all people! I'm sure you don't care about how I am; if anything, you want me DEAD!"

"Marduk," Dr Roberts spoke up. "It would be very easy for us to hate you; that would be the normal, natural thing to do. But our God is bigger than our feelings, and He has commanded us to be kind to our enemies, and to do good to those who do treat us badly. When we treat you kindly and serve you, we are serving our Lord and Savior; He, then, is our source of love for you.

And with that, Marduk drifted off into a painful sleep.

Marduk's confused mind drifted off into a dream. He dreamt that he heard the methodic pounding of nails, being driven into the hands and feet of a Man. Marduk heard the screams and incantations of the people who stood around Him, all full of accusations that angered him, making him feel that the Man deserved what He was getting. . But then he had looked into the Man's eyes, and saw no hatred or malice, but saw in them a sense of profound peace.

"Father, forgive them" he heard Him say, "for they don't know what they are doing." And He looked down at them all with the same forgiving, loving look that he had seen in the eyes of the Followers, who were looking down at him on the floor, and trying to find ways to help him.

It was the burning sensation of post-operative pain and the light-headedness due to excessive blood-loss that awakened Marduk for a second time, the day after his ordeal. When he slowly opened his eyes, he saw the figure of a woman. He thought he was dreaming, but the excruciating pain that he felt as he tried to sit up assured him that he was not.

She was standing in front of him; he was still lying down, now on a mattress on the ground in his lab. The woman came towards him slowly, hoping that she would not awaken him, but then she noticed that he was already awake. She knelt down beside him and gave him a drink of water from a small plastic bottle that she had. He noticed that in the other hand she held a sopping wet rag that she used to pat his forehead.

He had never experienced such kindness in his whole life. He was used to a society that did not care about him, or anybody else. The life he knew was madness, vengeance, and war; but the life of the Followers that he was now seeing was of love, forgiveness, and peace.

Marduk looked up and saw his reflection in a bit of unbroken glass on the wall; all the broken glass had been removed from his skin, and his wounds had been neatly dressed. His eyes flooded with tears, as he looked into the glass, and saw the genuine kindness that we had shown him. Even after what he had put us through, we were caring for him with an unnatural tenderness and sincerity. He felt guilty; and just as the Bible says; our kindness was as "heaping burning hot coals upon his head" and he felt bitterly ashamed.

As Dr. Roberts stooped down to examine his condition, Marduk spoke up. "Who are you? WHAT are you? How can you love me, who was experimenting harshly on you? Why are you doing this? Are you getting me better, so that you can experiment on me?"

"Forgive me, sir, for not introducing myself. My name is Dr. Roberts, and I was called to your aid. And no, I am not going to kill you. Jesus, my Lord and Master, has instructed us to do good to those who do us harm, and to love those who persecute us."

"Jesus? I've heard about Jesus. But I've always been taught that Jesus was a myth, an untruth, made up by weak men as a crutch."

"Believe me. It took a lot more strength for me to help you, rather than to kill you, as would have been the natural thing to do!"

Marduk then spoke up, and asked the most important question that he ever asked his whole life; "And where could I get this strength which you have, Dr. Roberts?" With that, Dr. Roberts knelt down to speak with Marduk. The rest of us stayed in the background and prayed for God's intervention.

Quietly Dr. Roberts asked Marduk, "Do you know what sin is?"

Marduk replied, "No, but I have a feeling that you are going to tell me."

"Sin is anything that we do that does not please God. Hatred, killing, and the worship of other gods; these are a few examples of things that displease God. God is the awesome force that brought everything into being. He made you, and he made me, deep in our mother's womb. From the beginning, God has been making a people for Himself. But man chose sin, and sinful ways, rather than what God had planned."

Dr Roberts continued, "There are many examples in the world we are living in today. In God's Word it says that ALL, including you and me, have sinned, and fall short of God's glorious ideal."

"God is love. That is who He is, more than simply what He does. God loves us; however, God, being holy and perfect, cannot accept sin. The punishment for sin is death."

Marduk nodded his head in agreement with the truth of what Dr. Roberts had said.

"Sin, as I said before, is anything that we do to displease God, and the punishment for sin is death, meaning eternal separation from God, or from good."

"How can I be forgiven, then, of my many sins?" Marduk asked repentantly.

"Ah yes." Dr. Roberts smiled broadly, "Here is where I find reason for living. God, our Creator, loves us. Regardless of our sin, He loves us. He showed us His love by sending His Son, Jesus Christ, to die in our place. But Christ was and is stronger than Satan. He is stronger than sin. He is stronger than death. After three days in the tomb, He rose again! Now He lives in Heaven defending us before His Father when we sin, reminding Him that He, our Savior Jesus Christ, has already paid the penalty for our disobedience and purchased our forgiveness. All we have to do is acknowledge our sin, confess to God that we are sinners, and accept Christ's forgiveness and His gift of eternal life."

"Would Jesus forgive even me?" Marduk stammered.

"Yes, by all means!" Dr. Roberts exclaimed enthusiastically. "Would you be interested in having your sins forgiven, and in starting to *really* live?"

"Yes, I would." Marduk whispered, tears forming in his eyes.

"Just simply repeat after me:

"Dear Lord,

I know I am a sinner. I know that I cannot save myself. I believe that Jesus died in my place, to forgive my sins. I believe in Christ, and I give him control of my life. By faith, I accept him as my Savior and Lord. Thank you, God, that You have helped me pass from death to life!

In Jesus' name,
Amen"

"Well, Marduk," Dr. Roberts smiled happily, extending his hand. "Welcome into the family of God! Christ, when he returned to Heaven, returned as King of Kings and Lord of Lords. He is preparing mansions for each of us in glory, where we will go after we die, to be with Him."

Marduk looked into the mirror again. He was still crying, but this time, crying for joy, a joy he had never felt before. Coupled with the joy was a peace of mind and heart because now he now had Jesus Christ as his Savior, and was indwelt by the Holy Spirit. That is what he wanted, and it would not ever be taken away from him.

4

Narrow Escape

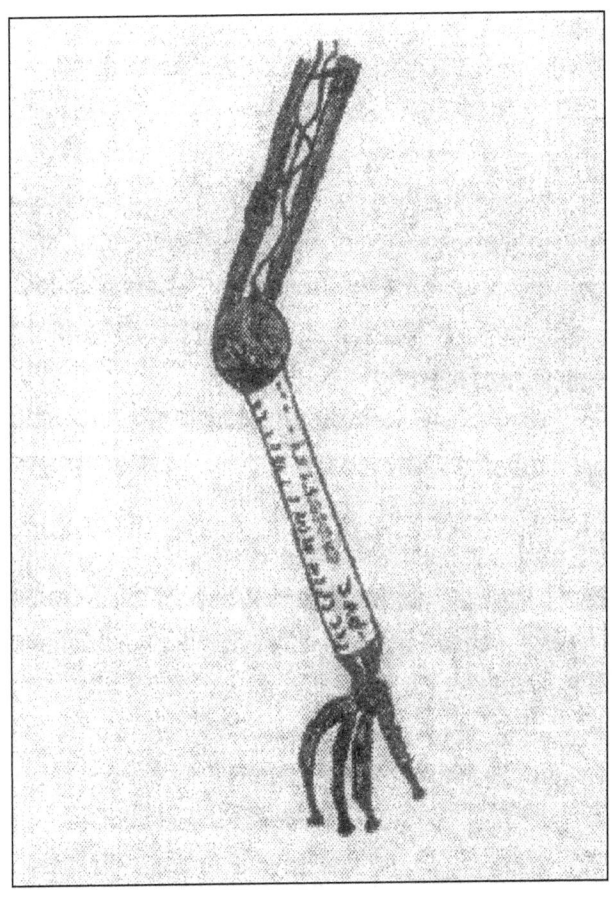

For the first couple days after his conversion, Marduk was very weak. He had lost a lot of blood, due to all the flying glass that had punctured his entire body, and the loss of his right leg from right above the knee.

Several days went by. Many times each day, Marduk worshipped his Savior with his newly acquired friends, even though we were the same people who had before been Marduk's guinea pigs, the people that he was using for his chemical experimentation. Now, however, we shared the same Holy Spirit, and had love for each other. This was a huge demonstration of the overwhelming power of God's love.

With the loss of his leg, Marduk also lost his ability to get around freely. It was Dr. Malerie who had the idea and came to Marduk with the plan. "Marduk, you know more than any of us about science. Why don't you use your ability to create for yourself a bionic artificial limb! If you have difficulty doing this, due to your lack of mobility, Dr. Roberts and I would be thrilled to help you!"

Marduk responded enthusiastically, "That is a wonderful idea! I can now use the same knowledge that before was used to take people's lives, to enhance my life, and to enable me to help others! Maybe when we get out of here, we can use our skills, your medical know-how and my scientific knowledge, to help other Followers or disabled people whom the Black Widows are attacking and abusing. It never dawned on me that I could use the same know-how that before was used for bad, for good!

"In His Word," Mrs. Roberts spoke up, "God tells us that 'all things work together for good for those who love Him and are called according to His purpose.'"

"Well," Marduk continued, "I can't think of a better time to start than right now! We'll need to have a clean, well-lit room to work in."

"I think this area over here might work," Sylvester called from the room that had been Marduk's lab during his service of the Legionnaire. It had a dirty sky-light over the table which would require considerable cleaning, since it had blood splattered on it, and was filthy. All the utensils were marred with grossness: dried blood, old pus, and gave off a putrid smell.

The whole room, for that matter, had not been cleaned for years, and required a lot of work, preparing it to be used as an operating room; we all worked together to ready it for its new purpose, and soon we were ready for Marduk to begin.

"Dr. Roberts, would you be able to reach up to that leg that is floating in the solution on the shelf in the room next door?" Marduk continued with his preparations for his first surgery. Glancing her way, he continued, "Dr. Malerie, would you please hand me the bits of metal and circuitry from the box on the table over there?"

Soon, the lab was buzzing with activity. Marduk used the metal and circuitry to form the bones and the joints for his prosthesis and then took the flesh and muscles from the part of the leg that had been amputated from another unfortunate soul to reconstruct a leg for himself.

Just as he was completing the final touches on the installation of the leg, Sylvester and I came running into the room yelling. "They're coming! The Black Widows! They're coming, and we had better get out of here quickly!"

Just then, we could hear the door off the corridor being blasted open, and we knew that our opportunity for escape was short. Marduk didn't have the luxury of trying out the leg, experimenting with it; it had to work, NOW!

Quickly, the four of us ran out, with one person on each of Marduk's arms to give him stability. into the adjacent room where Marduk had before had his secret lab, and slid the door shut behind us.

The Black Widows under the leadership of Spite, whose imagination and way of thinking was only evil personified, ran into the lab. When they entered, they could see that Marduk had recently been there, doing an experiment, or something. The utensils were still warm from his hands, so they knew for a fact that he could not be too far away.

The thing that surprised the Black Widows was that the lab was clean, and Marduk's lab was NEVER clean.

"Apparently he is still at work on something," one of Spite's assistants spoke up out of the silence. They quickly began searching for Marduk, mistakenly thinking that he was still working for them.

Three of the Black Widows ran outside to scope out the place, checking to see if there were any signs of where he had gone. "I don't know where he could be! I had wanted to hear what was done with those annoying Followers." Spite, perturbed, spat on the ground in disgust.

Inside Marduk's secret inner-lab, we Followers were baffled about what we should do.

"I have an idea!" Marduk whispered enthusiastically. "Before I aligned myself with Christ, I used this chemical to cause the Followers I was experimenting on to fall asleep, so that I could work with less difficulty. This liquid chemical, when shaken up, becomes a gas that has the same affect. Let's shake it up, and expel it through this hole into the front lab."

When the Black Widows were all inside the lab, we shook up the chemicals, and dispersed them through the hole in the wall. By this time all the Black Widows were inside. As the chemical spread throughout the room, they began feeling shortness of breath, and heavy eyelids. Spite said, "Is this just me, or are any of you getting tired, too?" With that, three of the Black Widows fell over, asleep, and Spite moved over to check on them. "Hey come on!" he said, and with that, fell over himself.

Marduk then removed the bottle from the hole and checked to see that all the Widows were asleep. "It's all clear now. They are out cold, but we had better move quickly, because the affects won't last for long, just about seven hours."

We moved swiftly, even boldly, into our old prison cell, and quickly grabbed what we really needed. Mrs. Roberts took her small New Testament, and the rest of us left ours there, so as to deceive the Black Widows better. We each had to leave behind our only pair of clean clothes. Dr. Roberts left a lot of his medical books behind. Dr. Malerie, with tears in her eyes, left behind most of the pictures that she had of her child as a newborn baby. Sylvester, who had been a policeman, had to leave behind his whistle, which had a good deal of sentimental value. I had to leave behind my writing material. Because I am a writer, I felt naked without it.

We each had to make our own sacrifice, in order to fool the Black Widows and not to be weighed down by non-essentials.

We knew that God would provide our every need, and our confidence in that fact helped us tremendously.

Our real treasures were laid up in Heaven. That gave us confidence in accepting the losses we were experiencing. We left the laboratory as soon as we had grabbed what we were going to be taking.

It may seem ironic that we were taking the very man who had been leading the persecution against us into our hiding place. Dr. Roberts shared with all of us that Marduk was going to be accompanying us on our escape from the Black Widows. The Holy Spirit confirmed in our hearts, however, that we were following His leading, and so we were at peace with it.

Mrs. Roberts was the first one to notice a historical parallel. "This is very much like the situation with the early church. We are being persecuted for our faith, just as the early church was persecuted for theirs. Saul of Tarsus was very involved in killing off the Followers of Christ. When he became a believer, however, his name was changed to Paul, and he lived, suffered, and died right along with them.

Simply imagine that we are located in the present day catacombs." When she said this, she was referring to a series of underground trails and small rooms found primarily in the south side of Chicago.

After Marduk's conversion, he lost interest in the making of weapons. He no longer was interested in taking lives, but instead, his chief concern was the bringing of life—eternal life—to a dying world.

Marduk wrote the Black Widows a letter explaining why he could no longer do the work of making weapons of death and destruction. He presented three basic points:

1. God made each one of us, and loves us. Recently, after my accident, I learned this truth, and accepted Christ, who is God's Son, as my personal Lord and Savior.
2. Christ told us to love each other, even as He did; He died for us!
3. Before, when I was so free about taking lives, it was because I myself had no real reason for living; now that I have found Christ, which I pray you will, too, my life has meaning, and I realize that everyone else's life does also.

When Spite and the Black Widows read the letter, they were even more enraged. They put out a warrant on Marduk, and issued a reward of $10,000 to anyone who could provide information as to his whereabouts, and $100,000 to anyone who would deliver his dead body to them.

Until now, the making of Liquid Death Missiles had been illegal for anyone other than Marduk. Therefore, the Black Widows were very serious in their attempts to find somebody to replace him.

Their search was fruitless, however. They could not find anybody who would admit to being able to do this. In their desperation, and not knowing how to contact Marduk, with embarrassment they resorted to the only means of communication that they could think of.

They posted the following note on every street light pole in the city:

> Dear Marduk,
>
> As your superior officer, I order you to resume your work of making destructive weapons. Not doing this could have serious consequences to both you and your friends. Do your job, or you'll find yourself dead. Anxiously waiting for your answer,
>
> Spite
> Leader of the Black Widows

Sylvester and I were out scrounging for food one night when I noticed the letter posted on a street light pole.

"Hey! What's this?" I read the message to him, and then Sylvester let out a quiet whistle.

"Wow," he said with a serious tone. "Another chance for God to prove himself faithful! Let's hurry up and get back to the others."

Quickly, I tore down the notice to show the rest of our group.

Upon our return, Marduk told us about some gruesome ways the Black Widows had of murdering people who did not comply with their demands. He said that once they cut an opponent's head open, removed his brain, and included it in a stew they were making.

On another occasion, after they had disemboweled one of their enemies, they pulled his guts out and showed them to him before cutting his head off.

So upon reading the letter, Marduk's first reaction was fear. Then he reasoned with himself; "Well, if I do not align myself with the Black Widows, I may loose my life. However, if I do not align myself with Jesus Christ, my Savior, I have lost my eternal life already!" That was when he decided what his decision would be and he wrote them the following reply:

> Dear Spite:
>
> I thank you for the invitation that you sent me. However, I still stand firm on my previous decision. I will make no more weapons. My decision is final, and is as solid as a rock, Christ Jesus, the Rock of my Salvation.
>
> Sincerely Yours,
> Marduk

As the clock struck twelve, Gruesome, who was the messenger agent who delivered the mail for the Black Widows, left his post in the Black Widows Crime Syndicate Building and ran out to his flying post-mobile. This was an extremely advanced mode of transportation about three meters long, and was made for one passenger at a time. It came to a point in the front, and was very sleek, allowing it to glide through the air with very little turbulence, and at a high rate of speed.

Simply the movement of one's body could affect the direction. If one desired to turn to the right, he would lean to the right; if he wanted to move to the left, he would lean to the left. For moving forward, he would lean forward, and to go backward, he would lean back. The bag of mail would be put in a compartment behind and under the seat.

Gruesome completed his task, and returned to the Black Widows Crime Syndicate Building. The whole building was very depressing to look at, dark and menacing, and human torches were used to light each floor. The building was a hexagon in shape and the windows were painted black. It was five stories high. Spite's headquarters were on the first floor. On the second, third, and fourth floors were BW Corners, where the Black Widows resided. On the fifth floor was a conference room, where Spite and the Black Widows would meet to plot and scheme ruthless and destructive activities.

As Gruesome climbed out of his flying post-mobile, Deathwish, Spite's agent, walked up to him and snarled, "What took you so stinking long? The Legionnaire wants to see you in his office, NOW!"

Gruesome snatched up the bag of mail and ran towards the Legionnaire's office. As he approached the door, he was hit with the potent smell of rotting flesh and stagnant blood. As he reached the doorknob, he saw that it was draped with veins.

"Gruesome!" The screeching voice of Spite filled Gruesome with shear terror, and he stammered back, "Here I am, Sir." "You're late again, and I won't stand for it!" With that, he pulled out his super-sonic hand cannon, and blasted Gruesome right there on the sidewalk where he stood.

Not wanting he same reception, Spite spun around and returned to his office. The walls of his office were dark red, having been painted with the blood of some of the Followers. The rug had been made with human hair. The cushion on the couch was of leather, but instead of being the hides of animals, it was made from the flesh of the Followers.

When Spite received Marduk's response, he was anything but happy with it. In fact, he was so enraged with Marduk that it was as if his blood was boiling in his veins. "That Marduk must die!!" he snarled. "Anyone who is not *for* us is *against* us. Speaking of rocks, I'd like to *stone* him!!"

"We must stop sitting around, waiting for others to find him," Spite yelled viciously. "Let's find him ourselves! I got word last night from the Legionnaire, saying that if we don't get this situation into control and do away with Marduk, the Legionnaire will take matters into his own hands, and do away with us!"

"Sir, I just thought of something that we should have thought of before." One of the Black Widows spoke up timidly. "We could use the Infra-Red X-ray Vision Laser-Scope and scan Chicagoland. Let's do it at night rather than during the day, because at night they will be less careful."

"Let's do it!" they said aggressively in unison.

"Great idea!" Spite exclaimed. " Let's vow that we will neither eat nor drink until Marduk is captured. And when that happens, let's celebrate! I want his head on a platter!"

* * *

In the same way as Paul had taken a leadership role in the church of his day, Marduk, who had natural leadership capabilities, as well as an informed knowledge of the Black Widows' schemes, kind of naturally became a leader, guiding the Followers in their escape.

The next day back in the tunnels, Marduk called an emergency meeting. "Brothers and sisters, we are not safe in this place." The Followers glanced at one another with a look of surprise and concern.

Dr. Malerie spoke up, voicing everyone's questions. "How do you know this, and if this is true, to where will we go? You know as well as I do that if we dare show our faces in society, we will all die."

Dr. Roberts answered Dr. Malerie's questions. "The neighborhood children have found the entrance to the tunnels, and have built a little fort there. In no time at all, they will begin exploring, and then our hideout will be exposed."

"Also, on one of my trips outside the catacombs searching for food, I heard the people saying that Marduk is a threat alive, and that he is better-off dead. Don't worry, though; God Himself will protect us from Spike's evil schemes."

"Christ promised never to leave us nor forsake us. He's with us, regardless of where we go, or what transpires," Sylvester added with conviction.

"But where are we all to go?" Mrs. Roberts asked.

"I don't know," Dr. Roberts responded. "Let's pray that God will provide a place that is safe for all of us. Even before we continue this conversation, I feel that we should pray, and invite Christ to direct us to the place that He wants."

"Amen to that!"

I spoke up. "May I pray?" After receiving their blessing, I bowed my head, and closed my eyes.

"Dear Lord,

Thank You for who You are. Thank You that You are our Great Provider; thank You that we are important to You; we are Your children. Lord, we need a place to stay. Presently there is a threat on our lives, and our hiding place has been discovered. We humbly ask for a place to live in safety, free from danger of those who desire to harm us. Please give us wisdom, and

a peace that passes understanding during this
fearful time.

In Your Son's name,

Amen"

Marduk had been quiet for a good while. He was sad-
dened that his being there had alerted the Black Widows to
the existence of the catacombs. That is when God reminded him. "Oh yeah!" Marduk shared enthusiastically, "Dr.
Roberts! I remember that underground, along the streets
in the older area of the city, is the antiquated drainage system."

"Good," Dr. Roberts said.

"Good thinking, Marduk. We don't have a minute to
lose. O.K. everybody, grab what you really need, but leave
some of our stuff here, to fool the Black Widows into thinking that we will be returning."

5

Our New Adventure

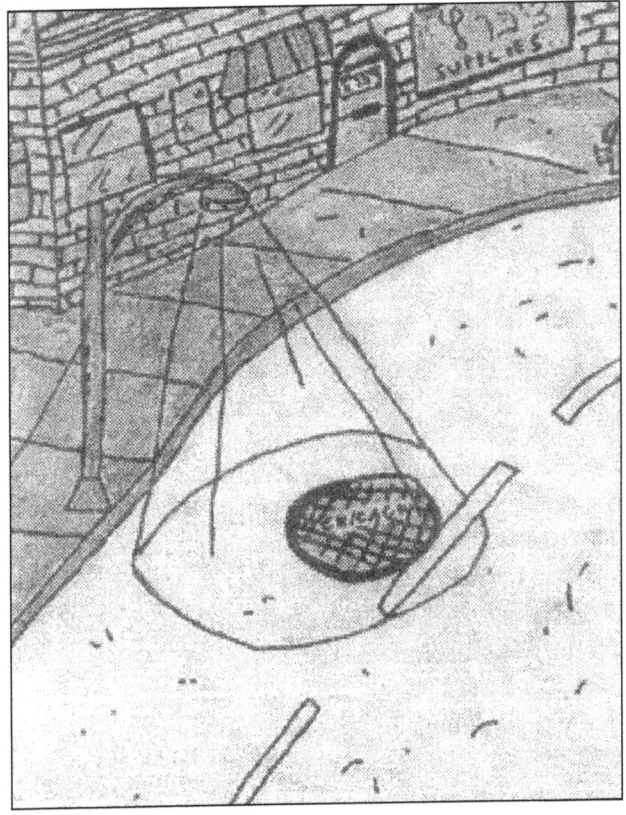

Because of his prior knowledge of the layout of the city, it's roadways and it's drainage system, and because of his experience in helping the Black Widows in matters such as their search for the Followers, Marduk was made to be the guide for the Followers' escape. He knew the search patterns of the Black Widows, and so he led us by different routes, and in unusual ways.

We went swiftly and quietly out the side door, and into the back alley that was seldom used. We walked briskly through the city, using the least occupied routes, trying not to call attention to ourselves. We walked in the alley-way for several hours, and soon, on both sides of us there were looming sky scrapers. The walkway began descending, as the speedway crossed over it.

When we reached the bottom of the descent, Marduk motioned to us to come to where he was standing. There in the wall was a metal gate, which hung on very squeaky hinges. At first, the gate refused to open and it looked like we were going to have to adopt another plan. Then Marduk remembered his bionic leg; this was the perfect time to put it to the test. He straightened up, reeled back, and gave the gate such an incredible kick that it banged open.

Marduk smiled as he saw the marveled expressions on everyone's face and chuckled to himself, "Well, in our study, you told me that God works everything together for the good of those who love Him. Here's a great example! I never would have been able to do that were it not for the fact that I had lost my leg, and had to replace it with a scientifically made prosthesis."

Dr. Malerie smiled and said. "Amen. Here is another incident of God working in mysterious ways, to perform His Wonderful plans."

"Where are we going?" Sylvester inquired.

Marduk answered, "This is the entrance into the old drainage system which has been out of commission for ages. A couple of years ago, the city was forced to clean it out, because of the toxic and flammable gases that were coming out of here.

The air itself is no longer dangerous, but please be extremely cautious, as the piping is in bad repair. At places there are holes that if one were to fall through, it could be fatal. The surface is slick, because of the slimy plankton, and it makes for difficult walking. Let's pray, and ask God for his loving hand of protection, as we embark on this next phase of our adventure."

With that, the Followers all formed a circle and held hands. Mrs. Roberts spoke up. "I have a Psalm that I would like to quote, as I think it is very applicable to the present moment.

The Lord is my Shepherd, I shall not want.
He maketh me lie down in green pastures.
He leadeth me beside still waters.
He restoreth my soul. He leadeth me in
   the paths of righteousness for His Name's sake.
Yea, though I walk through the valley of
   the shadow of death,
I will fear no evil, for Thou art with me.
Thy rod and Thy staff, they comfort me.
Thou preparest a table before me in
   the presence of mine enemies,
Thou anointest my head with oil;
My cup runneth over
Surely goodness and mercy shall follow me
   all the days of my life,
   and I will dwell in the house of the Lord forever."

After the group had quoted the Psalm together Dr. Roberts asked if he could lead us in prayer. We all nodded in approval, and Dr. Roberts began . . .

"Dear Lord,

Thank you for being our rock and our fortress, a very present help in time of trouble. We look into the Bible, and see so many times when You proved Yourself faithful to Your followers. We consider how You proved to be true to Noah and Moses, Daniel and Esther, Peter and Paul, and all the rest of those who believed in You. Lord, You are the only true God, and we are privileged to be enduring this little bit of hardship for You. We request, Lord, that You would go before us now, into this abyss. Please protect us from the potential dangers that lie ahead, and from the power of the evil one. We put this whole circumstance into Your almighty hands, seeking for your guidance, protection, and peace. Thank you that you 'never leave us nor forsake us.'

In Jesus' name we ask it,
Amen"

With that, Marduk whispered into my ear, and I spoke up.

"Hey, you guys, It's getting late. The sun is going down and we are still very much exposed if anybody were to come back here. Come on! Let's get going before the Black Widows come and find us!"

"Watch your heads!" Marduk yelled back. The entrance to the drainage pipes was very narrow and low to the ground, so we had to get down onto our knees and crawl through awkwardly.

Glancing at Mrs. Roberts, who had a very 'broad beam,' Sylvester commented, "Do you think that we are all going to be able to *fit* through that little hole?" He smiled jokingly, and Mrs. Roberts rolled her eyes back at him.

"Well," Mrs. Roberts responded with a grin, "I *think* I can, I *think* I can. And if I have any troubles with it, I'm glad that I can count on you to give me a shove, Sylvester."

Meanwhile, the Black Widows finally woke up from their sleep. They had been out cold for seven hours. When he came to, Spite's head was spinning.

"Hey! What happened?" Looking around, Spite saw his men, strewn out on the floor in various forms of disarray. At first his memory of what had happened was very sketchy; the major thing he could recall was that Marduk was missing.

He could also remember a strange gas coming from a hole in the wall; the cleanliness of the lab was another thing that was so different from usual, he could not forget it.

"Come on men, get up!" Spite prodded the men with the brunt of his laser machine gun.

"Let's go find Marduk, get our job done, and get out of here!" Spite salivated as he spoke these words, and spat on the ground.

One of the Black Widows whose name was Blaze walked over to the wall from which the gas had come, and began inspecting it closely. He knocked on it, and when it gave a hollow sound, it gave him the clue that there was a room behind it.

As he ran his fingers over the surface, he bumped the trigger, and the door swung open a little bit. "Look what I found! It's some sort of opening!"

With that the Black Widows all ran over to the wall, yanked the door open violently, exposing Marduk's experimental lab that they had not realized was there. "Wow!" exclaimed Spite. With that, the Black Widows cautiously entered the experimental lab, investigating every corner with their X-ray Infra-Red Laser-Beamed Flashlights.

Spite was using his human bioscanner, looking for life signs other than his own or those of his party. Finding none, aside from rats, he grunted in frustration and spat on the ground.

"Well, you fools! Have you found nothing, yet?" Spite glared intensely at Blaze. "What do I pay you for, you worthless fool?" Spite struck him, so hard that it left marks on Blaze's face.

Venting his anger, Blaze responded, "Speak for yourself! Have you found anything? I was the one who found this room!"

Spite retaliated violently. "I've had enough of your lip!" With that, he slugged Blaze across the face with such tremendous force that it sent him whimpering into the corner like a whipped dog. "This is what will happen to any of you if you don't bring me Marduk when I ask for him. Bring him NOW!"

"Sir! We have found a door!" Snake yelled from the corner. As the others approached the dark passageway, the rancid smell almost knocked them off their feet. In fact, the odor was so unpleasant that the Black Widows had to put on their compounded energy oxygen masks.

Suspecting an ambush by Marduk, Spite pulled out his Grade Ten Laser-Fast Gun, and loaded it with five explosive platinum bullets; the others all pulled out their hand-held Laser Canons. Cautiously and silently, they began their descent down the eerie, narrow, dark hallway.

Looking into his Human Bioscanner, Spite could not see any humans. Upon arriving to the last cell, they found all the belongings that we had left behind.

Grave, the expert in mental human tactics, replied, "Sir, I suspect that we have been tricked, been made fools of, sir."

In response, Spite angrily clenched his teeth, shook his fists violently, and aimed his gun at Grave's head. In his fury, he pulled the trigger and Grave let out a shriek of agony, as the bullet took effect. His flesh liquefied and melted like wax on a candle, exposing his skeletal make-up, turning into nuclear atomic dust.

In rage, Spite whirled around and glared with malice at the other Black Widows who were accompanying him. "Now that" he hissed angrily, "is exactly what will happen to all of you if you do not hurry up and find Marduk." Spite spat on the ground, and kicked with disgust at the atomic dust, creating a dirty cloud of their co-worker's remains.

"Let's get out of here!" Spite barked at his men. "Obviously the Followers have left here! Let's search through the whole city, leaving no stone unturned." With that, Spite and his men thundered out of the laboratory, resembling a herd of buffalo.

To begin with, the Black Widows were simply running hither and yon, looking into every possible hiding spot, some of which were looked at two or three times, by different agents.

Finally, Spite called to the Black Widows, saying, "We must have a meeting tonight to determine what our plan of attack will be for this search, to prevent the waste of time, which is important, and to save energy."

Blaze then bravely spoke up. "May I make a suggestion, sir?"

"What!?!" Spite snapped.

"Maybe we could use our heat detecting, X-ray Scope to discover where the Followers are hiding."

"For once, you have come up with a good idea." This was as close to a compliment that Blaze would ever hope to hear from Spite, who was not known for praising anybody but himself. "Let's plot out the layout of the city, so that we will know who is going where. That way we will not be covering the same area more than once."

With that, Spite pulled a computer chip out of his shoulder pocket, and popped it into the mini-computer that he had imbedded in his forearm. In the next few moments the city was mapped out, and a section given to each of the Black Widows. "OK, you may go now, but remember. If they get by you, I'm holding YOU responsible. Also, remember to maintain open communication throughout the search."

6

Evil Foe's Demise

MEANWHILE, MRS. Roberts was having a very difficult time of it. Now she'd been in a tight squeeze before, but never anything that could compare with the current situation. In her present dilemma. she was running for her life, but trying to be as invisible as possible. At every turn, she was uncertain as to whether or not she would come face to face with her opposition. They were even uncertain as to whether the destination of their running would be safe or not.

Mrs. Roberts way of responding to the stress of it all was a bit unconventional. She grunted. She groaned. She wriggled. She squirmed. Finally, she let out a long sigh and said to her companions, "Listen folks, please pray again with me for God's help, and for His peace. He shut the lion's mouths for Daniel, saved Jonah from the whale, and helped Peter walk on water. I have no doubt that he can squeeze us through this tight situation, also!"

With that, we all bowed our heads, I held her hand, and we prayed for God's help. After we had finished, Silvester exclaimed, "Here's one more try!" And with that, he pushed from the outside, while Marduk pulled from the inside. All of a sudden it was as if Mrs. Roberts popped out of the entrance like a cork out of a champagne bottle, and into the main drainage pipe. She and Marduk rolled over a couple of times. Suddenly Marduk cried, "Ouch!" With that, he reached down to feel what he had hit his head against, and found a large rectangular metal box.

With curiosity he reached out to examine what the box was. It was an old trunk, quite heavy, and with the light from his flashlight he saw that it had "Stefan Stevens" written on a neon-yellow sticker, with jet black lettering. Marduk let out a low moan and Dr. Roberts whistled quietly.

"My goodness! Do you remember who Stefan Stevens was?! He was a martyr for the Follower faith way back in 1976! What could God have led him to leave here, for us?" With that question vivid on everybody's mind, they scrambled to open the trunk. The men tried to get the lock open, but it was to no avail. The huge lock seemed to be an insurmountable barrier.

Then Mrs. Roberts again made her gentle reminder; "Marduk, brothers, let's pray about it. God wouldn't put the trunk here if it was outside of His plan to help us." Everybody was quick to agree, and in the middle of their prayer, Dr. Malerie felt a strange tickling at the back of her head, and as she went to scratch it, she felt a bobby pin in her hair.

"Hey men! Would this help?" she asked excitedly.

"Maybe this is how God plans to help us. Hand it to me, please." Marduk took the metal clip and bent it. Putting it into the lock, he steadied himself and turned it. The clicking sound echoed through the tunnel, and everyone responded with an excited, "Praise God!" Our enthusiastic praise resounded through the pipe.

With that, the lid of the old trunk began to open and a strange, florescent blue light came out of it, mysteriously lighting the dark, damp surroundings. With curiosity and bewilderment Dr. Roberts exclaimed, "And what do we have here?"

As soon as he had voiced the question that was plaguing all of our minds, Silvester spotted five computer disks in the bottom of the trunk.

"Yo!" He said, "And what do we have here?!" Bending over, he grabbed from the inside of the trunk five triangular armored-steel disks, turned them over in his hands a couple of times, and blew centuries of dust off of their surfaces.

At that moment, Marduk looked at me and pointed to a hexagon-shaped mechanism that was also in the trunk, exclaiming, "I never would have imagined that the scientists and inventors were so mechanically advanced way back in Stefan's time, 1976!

We have always considered that period of time to be very primitive and undeveloped in regards to technology and scientific breakthroughs. Obviously we were wrong!

Let's try to learn how to work this device that we have found."

It took us a while to examine and figure out the pieces of forgotten technology, but, in time, Marduk and I uncovered the secrets of this centuries-old communication device.

As we looked at the communicator, we wondered what the source of energy would be. Opening the hexagonal-shaped computer, we found three differently formed slots. In the bottom of the trunk, we found three differently facetted gem-stones, who's shapes matched those in the computer

When they were put in place, the gemstones started to glow, and the computer began to buzz. As we entered one of the disks, the blue light flickered and made a crackling sound as the computer turned on.

"Hello, fellow Believers." The voice spoke, but the speaker could hardly be seen or understood, due to the immense static. Marduk twisted a few knobs on the hexagonal computer, and the three dimensional electronically-powered life form cleared, as did the audio.

Stefan continued, "I was told that you would be in your present predicament long before you were even born, and God gave me these tools to share with you, to help you in combating the evil that is presently confronting you. As you can see, there are five triangular armored-steel disks, each of which will aid you in combating and defeating your oppressors, and in fulfilling your ministry of love among the people. Remember, God Himself is the source of all strength, and He even was the provider of the help which I am passing on to you now.

"This first disk will be useful for your safety at the present time. The Black Widows will come and find you at any moment, but you will notice that the blue light is having a strange affect on the space in this drainage system."

"Wow! Look over here!" It was Silvester yelling in disbelief. As we turned hastily to look at what he was pointing to, we saw that the blue light seemed to be dividing reality itself; everything that was above the light was turning up, and everything that was below was turning down.

Between these two realms there was an opening in space that at first was very misty and dark, but as soon as the mist settled, we could see that God Himself had caused a division in reality. There was a parting, you might say, revealing a place where we could hide from the Black Widows.

"The second disk will send out such a high pitch that it will not be audible to human ears, but it will cause confusion to the brain signals of androids. In case you did not know, with the exception of Spite, who is human, and Blaze, who is half human, half android, the Black Widows are all androids who were designed by Spite himself."

At that time I said to Marduk, "Do you mean to tell me that all that time you were taking your orders from measly machines?!"

"Believe me, Victor, those androids are anything but measly! Androids are made of Mikazorconakite, which is an extremely durable and strong metal, and they are able to respond with lightening speed; each of them has the strength of twenty men, with their compounded energy reserves. Each one of them have embedded in their eardrums an ultra-sensitive microphone which enables them to hear the smallest sound from a great distance. Their eyes have miniature cameras embedded in them, and they are able to replay incidents that they see. Although they look human, since they have human flesh, they are not and are heartless, without mercy."

"The third disk will be your camouflage," Stefan continued. "It will help conceal your hiding places and will help you adapt to your surroundings. As He was for the Israelites in the times of old, God desires to be your rock and your fortress, a very present help in times of trouble." Move quickly now, and put your belongings and yourselves into the hiding place. The other two disks must also be inserted into their appropriate slots."

At that, the figure of Stefan faded and in its place we could see the televised images of the Black Widows approaching the entrance to the drainage system. With our belongings, we rushed to the entrance of the God-given hide-out and climbed into it. Mrs. Roberts required a few of us men to push, and a couple to pull, getting her up the big step into our new hide away and home.

Quickly, we set up the hexagonal computer and inserted the third disk, which was our camouflage. We could see a strange light beginning to surround us and we knew that we were now invisible. We were still able to see out of the hidden area and we watched as the Black Widows entered the drainage system. They were looking directly as us, yet not seeing us. We all held our breath.

Dr Roberts put his arm around his wife and held her close so that she would feel safe. Once, as Dr. Malerie, who was holding her crying infant up close to her breast, saw one of the Black Widows looking right towards her, she gasped. We were all afraid that she and her daughter had blown our cover. Silvester quickly drew his shaking wife over to his side and hugged her in his loving arms.

The Black Widow did not seem to know or understand where the noise had come from and he had a puzzled look on his face. Then Marduk quickly inserted the second disk. As soon as the disk began to work, the heads of the

Black Widows all suddenly jerked up violently, and turned quickly from side to side.

"What is this?!" Spite yelled angrily, and spat on the ground. Torn between being both man and machine, Blaze's face began to twist and contort. Because of the sudden, unexpected stress, the flesh on the face of Blaze began to curl up on the Android side, exposing the parts of his skull that were made of Mikazirconakite.

Screaming in agony, Blaze could feel his android brain cells fusing together into clumps, as he felt his mental capacities diminishing. He held his hands to his temples, and began rocking his head back and forth, hoping to alleviate the mysterious torture that he was undergoing.

His robotic eyes began flickering uncontrollably, and the metallic shell to his brain began to melt, and then to ooze out of his ears. Blaze began panting, as one would do after a hard run, and each time he exhaled, his breath came out as a puff of smoke.

As the second disk wailed, the effects on each of the Black Widows were all different, but each equally as deadly. Some of them began to heat up drastically. They turned bright red, then orange, then yellow because they were composed primarily of Mikazirconakite. They melted, forming pools of slippery metal on the floor of the drainage pipe.

Others completely lost their minds. They began zooming through the pipes, not taking notice of the holes in the antiquated piping. Just one misguided footstep, and they fell screaming to their deaths.

Some were consumed with hatred and began shooting violently at each other; others, in a homicidal rampage, began ripping and tearing each other apart.

Regardless of how it happened, in about ten short minutes, the only Black Widows who were left alive were Spite and a badly damaged Blaze. Because the Black Widows had been his own creation, Spite felt at quite a loss, also. Feeling that this was all on account of the Followers, although he could not put his finger on "how" they had done it, he was overcome with an added, new, even deeper hatred and resentment for the Followers of Christ.

Blaze and Spite sulkily staggered out of the drainage pipe. We Followers, who were all drenched in sweat and had been almost holding our breath in suspense, all exhaled at once and exclaimed, "Praise God!" in unison. "Wow!" I said, "Isn't God Creative! Who would have thought that He would use a dead scientist from 1976, and an old-fashioned computer, and a "dividing reality" to save us?!"

"Whew! For a minute there, I was sure they had us!" As she exclaimed this, Malerie glanced at her baby. Silvester responded, "I've heard of the scream of death before, but I've never experienced it quite like that!

Just then, Mrs. Roberts spoke up. "I think we've forgotten something, don't you? We haven't given thanks to God yet, for saving us."

Marduke spoke up. "Mrs. Roberts, I can think of nobody more deserving of the honor of praying for us than yourself, as through-out our difficult situation, you have maintained our dependence on Christ, the Rock of our Salvation."

With that, Mrs. Roberts said, "Let's hold hands in a circle."

"Dear God, Our Father,

Thank you for Your Presence through the difficult situation that we have been in. Regardless of what we were experiencing, we could know with certainty that You were with us, and that you were Greater than the oppressors. Thank You for giving Stephan the forethought to leave for us, in the tunnel, all that we needed for safety. The knowledge to do that could have come from You alone. Thank you for not only keeping us safe, but also for almost obliterating our enemies.

Once again, Father, thank You that Marduk is now on our side, on Your side, and is helping us to fight the evil one.

Thank You for each one of my friends, my family in the faith, whom I can go through this experience with. Thank You that we can be helpers for each other, and I thank You for the unity that we feel in Christ Jesus our Lord and Savior.

Thank You, thank You, thank You! And all God's people said . . ." and we all joined in unison, "AMEN!"

7

Life Found in Death

L IFE, HOWEVER, was not nearly so promising for Spite and Blaze. When the two of them slumped out of the drainage system, both of them felt exhausted, damaged, and distraught. Blaze was completely malformed.

Spite was experiencing great pain, but he was also sick with hatred for the Followers, whom he was certain were responsible for the destruction of all but one of his creations, his army. All the years of his work was gone in the blink of an eye. The harsh reality crept in; then he had to deal with reality as it was. Blaze, his number one man, was dying.

At first, Spite was tempted to begin work on remaking Blaze's face, as it was grotesquely malformed, but quickly he realized that the appearance was the least of his concerns. Blaze's vital functions were so critically impaired that he was now breathing unevenly, and his heartbeat was faltering.

Spite took him to the lab where he had created him, and tried replacing his faulty body parts, attempting to simply keep Blaze alive long enough to complete the process needed to revive him, but it was to no avail. In the end, Spite made an error, a fatal miscalculation, short circuiting Blaze's Android motor functions.

In an instant, there was a loud crackling sound and then immediately following that, his eyes shattered, splintering in every direction. The tubes in Blaze's brain began filling up with air and exploding. His brain matter splattered on Spite's face.

Suddenly flames roared out of Blaze's mouth, nose, eyes, and ears. Almost instantaneously Blaze's clothing caught fire, and before it could be removed, the oil that was on his mechanized joints burst into flames. This only quickened the cremation process. At that point, Blaze was nothing more than a blaze.

Spite began to wail in deep sobs, not only because of the pain that he was experiencing, but also because Blaze had been his creation. He had ended up causing Blaze's death, rather than his recuperation. Spite was devastated. He cried out in anger; he screamed in dismay; he clawed at his face in agony.

Thoughts of suicide entered his mind, but he quenched them quickly, realizing that suicide would solve nothing.

Instead, he began meditating on what he could do to bring about revenge for his creation's death.

Spite was consumed with his hatred for the Followers, to the extent that vengeance colored his every waking thought, and tainted his meditation upon retiring in the evening.

The desire for revenge, and his complete malice for the Followers, put a foul taste in his mouth, and gave him a razor-sharp pain in the pit of his stomach.

Now Spite stood alone. After the death of Blaze, Spite's hatred for the Followers and for the God they served hit an all-time low. It was made even worse, because strangely, the Followers did not mirror his hatred. Instead they responded to him in love. This gave validity to all that they were saying, and that did not make Spite happy. This was not the thing he had expected.

At this time, Marduk called a meeting of all the Followers.

"Men and women, or make that brothers and sisters," he continued.

"As you can see, Satan has been and is on the attack. Don't loose heart though, because remember; when Christ arose from the dead, He defeated him. He has been conquered already, and guess what? We are on the winning side!

"I will admit that my first inclination is to want to hate Spite. But hatred is not the way God works; the Lord's tactic, as displayed on the cross, is love. Let's love Spite into the Kingdom.

Remember what the Bible says," Marduk continued, "Love your enemies, and do good to them that hate you. Blessed are those of you who are persecuted for My Name's sake, for theirs is the kingdom of Heaven."

"Do you mean to tell me that we are supposed to LOVE that creep?" One of the newer Christians spoke up from the group.

"Believe me, right at this moment my natural attitude would be to do *anything* but good to Spite, but let's all come together and pray that God will give us hearts of love for him." And with that, the followers of Christ all bowed their heads, closed their eyes, and spoke to the God who could take their hatred, and replace it with a love that only originates with Him.

Then Marduk reminded them all, "By the way, do you all remember who I am, and what my job used to be? God has changed me, and I mean completely, into being His child. I once was working hard to abolish His name from the face of the earth, and now I am willing to sacrifice my life for it! God can take Spite, also, and make the same transformation in him, if that would be in His plan."

"It is so easy to forget that, Marduk!" I exclaimed. "Look at all that God has done in remolding you! You're not the same person that you were only seven months ago."

Dr. Malerie then spoke up. "God *is* in the business of transforming people and personalities, isn't He?"

"You've got that right!" Silvester exclaimed. "I hate to remember what I was. I was a man chained with bitterness, and malice was my middle name."

"I can remember that most of my time was consumed by anxiety; worrying about Dr. Roberts, fretting about the weather; wondering in fear about what we would eat, or drink, or wear," Mrs. Roberts continued. "All of us have experienced worry, but look at us now! Thanks be to God, He has taken all of our preoccupation, because we have put our lives into His almighty hands. He is bigger than our problems."

"Amen to that!" Dr. Roberts chimed in enthusiastically.

"How do you think we can demonstrate love to Spite?" I asked inquisitively.

"Well, we are going to have to be moving from place to place, in order to remain in hiding. Maybe we could leave behind a note for him at each hiding spot, restating to him that we love him and want to forgive and be rejoined with him. We could include with each note scripture that deals with the forgiveness of God. That is where true reconciliation begins."

* * *

Several weeks went by, and at each hiding place, when we moved on to the next, we would leave behind a different verse on a note to Spite which spoke about the forgiveness which God desired to give him.

"He (God) forgives (pardons) all my sins (the bad things I do), and heals all my diseases." (Psalm 103:3)

". . . want you to know that through Jesus the forgiveness of sins is proclaimed to you." (Acts 13:38)

"If we confess our sins (wrong-doings), He is faithful and just and will forgive us our sins and purify us from all unrighteousness." (I John 1:9)

Spite found the hiding places, because each time, as we were leaving our place of refuge, we would leave many obvious signs, to ensure that he would uncover it. Each time, as Spite discovered these little messages, instead of making him desire to commune with us, it fueled his anger against us all the more.

Spite continued his search for us for the next five months. We were not being secretive about our faith, but were holding open-air meetings, and were boldly declaring to the people the foolishness of putting their faith in a mere person such as the Legionnaire, or in buildings or monuments.

"These are simply creations of men," we told them. We taught them about the loving, all-powerful God, who had a divine plan for each one of them.

Many of the people were quick to acknowledge the stupidity of worshipping silly Monuments, which they themselves had made. They could see in the people who worshipped "the Lord Jesus" a power that was not imaginary, and did not have its source in the Followers themselves.

They saw a supernatural love in the Followers of Jesus that did not seem to be just simply man-made, but instead seemed to be God-given. They saw a strength and endurance that came from someplace other than the Followers themselves.

The number of people who joined the Followers in worshipping Christ Jesus grew every day and the numbers who were denouncing their previous ways of life to follow this "Christ-man" overwhelmed Spite. He decided that he would once-and-for-all teach the Followers something that they would not easily forget.

One day, Marduk and I were witnessing to a large crowd of people in the park that ran alongside the lake. Spite wove himself quietly into the crowd, and stealthily made his way closer and closer to the front.

Suddenly, he came running up and jumped onto the stage. He grabbed Marduk by the throat, and with his pistol aimed at Marduk's head, he motioned to me and pushed Marduk to the back of the stage.

At gunpoint, he led us down the stairs, and into his winged black hover-mobile, which he had positioned there. The crowd gasped, but before anybody could do anything,

Spite bound our wrists securely and sped away with the two of us deeply sedated by the drugs that he had administered to us.

Quickly, Spite took us to his secret hide-away, a dreary, damp cave that was positioned in the side of a mountain. When we arrived there, he woke us up by slapping us across the face with his sweaty palm, and in his gruff voice he directed us up the steep incline to a well-concealed entrance.

Spite then carelessly pushed us down the darkened hallway. Our hands were firmly tied behind our backs. After spitting in my face in disgust, he shoved me into a narrow cell.

But before Spite had the chance to slam the door behind me, I called out to Marduk, "Remember Marduk, Christ said, 'I will never leave you nor forsake you.'"

8

Unexpected Relationships

ANGRILY, SPITE pushed Marduk down the darkened hall to his prison stall.

"Well, you idiot, what are you going to say for yourself?! You've gotten all mushy about this Jesus guy. You seem to have forgotten who you are working for; you're working for ME, right?"

"No," Marduk responded with a peaceful smile on his face. "I don't work for you anymore. When I did work for you, my job was based on hatred and revenge. My eyes were turned inward, and I was extremely depressed.

"After I was injured there in the lab, even though the accident occurred while I was in the process of killing the Followers of Jesus, they came alongside me, and cared for me with a love that I had never before experienced. They loved me, their killer.

"They were showing me a love that does not begin with themselves, but rather it has its origin in Christ, who gave himself to die for our sins so that we could be forgiven and live triumphantly in Him."

"Shut up!" Spite was overcome with hatred of this Jesus whom he felt had allowed for his family to be murdered. Any God who was really in control of the universe would never have allowed his Followers to be killed in such an awful fashion.

"You are so delusional; you have deceived yourself, and now you are deceiving others as well. This has got to stop or you'll corrupt more people with your stupid ideas."

Then, putting his rapid-fire Laser Pistol up to Marduk's head, he shouted, "All right, the choice is yours. Either you renounce your faith in this Jesus dude, and tell me that it was just a figment of your imagination, or I'll splatter your brains against the wall with one blast of my gun."

Marduk then looked into Spite's face, and without flinching, said, "Spite, you can blow me up, burn me to a crisp, chop me up in pieces, or whatever you want to do; but the fact remains the same. Christ is alive; He has changed my life completely, giving it a meaning it never had before.

"Death no longer has the same sting for me; when I die now, I simply know that I'll be with Jesus in Heaven! 'For me to live is Christ, and to die is gain.'"

At this moment, Spite detested Marduk even more than before. Although it was not until after he himself had changed that he realized it, he was very jealous of Marduk. Death petrified him, but it didn't even seem to faze Marduk.

The other believers were very concerned about the well being of Marduk and me. Many had been present at the meeting when Spite had suddenly appeared and taken us hostage. They had seen him bind our hands and then push us into the black winged Hovercraft. The last they had seen of us had been when Spite had put the gun with the sleeping drug up to our necks and fired it.

Everyone was overcome with concern. This included not only the Followers, but also the huge number of Chicagoans who were present. People started buzzing and reminding each other about how vicious Spite was. That was when Mrs. Roberts went over and whispered something into her husband's ear.

"Men and women," Dr. Roberts yelled loudly, "my wife has just reminded me that we have forgotten one very important thing. God is in control of all of this; I don't have the foggiest idea what He's doing right now, but praise God, He does!

"We don't need to stoop to Spite's level, and respond with hatred. Let's go to Him and voice our concern, and request for the safe release of those men, if that would be in His perfect will. Also, let's pray for Spite himself. He is an extremely unhappy person, and is consumed by vengeance.

"We all know, however, the author of love, joy, forgiveness and everything that is good. Let's pray with earnestness that God will open Spite's eyes, and that he will accept the forgiveness and wholeness that comes only in Christ Jesus."

With that, we all closed our eyes, and Dr. Roberts prayed.

> "Holy Father,
>
> We thank You that You are in control right now. Please forgive us for beginning to be overwrought with concern and worry about the well being of our friends. We realize now that You are in control over everything and we simply need to leave it all in Your all-powerful hands. Please grant safety to Victor and Marduk; it would be wonderful, Lord God, if You would even use this situation to bring Spite to Yourself! He needs You desperately, just as each of us need You, and rejoice in the God of our Salvation.
>
> In your Son Jesus' name,
> Amen"

After he had prayed, all the Followers felt real peace. The non-Followers, or in many cases the pre-Followers, were overwhelmed with how much faith in his God Dr. Roberts demonstrated.

Mrs. Roberts had the idea of instigating a rescue plan, although at that time they were not sure if we were dead or alive. In frustration, Silvester exclaimed, "I don't know where to start! I don't have the foggiest idea of where Spite is hiding now-a-days."

That was when one of the new Followers of Jesus, a young man named Peter, spoke up. "I think that I can help. Over on the east side of the city close to the lake there is a small mountain or hill. I've seen Spite lingering around that spot quite a bit. The other night, even as I was watching, it seemed that the mountain kind of swallowed up Spite's black-winged Hovercraft, including the passengers who were with him.

In my opinion, I think that it would be a good idea to start there in our search. I'd be willing to lead you guys; it might be a good idea for some of us to stay behind, though, in case Spite should appear again."

At that moment, one of the other men who had just accepted Christ said, "I was a policeman before I was made to become a Monument builder, so I have a couple of walkie-talkies that you may use, if you want, to be able to maintain communication between groups."

It was a young, athletic teenager who spoke up next. "I'm pretty quick on my feet. I used to be involved in track and field at school, before schools were made obsolete. I would love to have the opportunity to use my skill to serve Jesus. Can I go along on the search?"

Silvester spoke up in answer to his question. "Sure. We welcome all of you who can come along, but Dr. Roberts and his wife will remain in case Spite returns. Also, we who are going will really appreciate the prayer support of those of you who stay behind."

At that point, Silvester took one of the walkie-talkies that had been offered to him, and handed it to Dr. Roberts. "Here. You take this and keep us notified about what is happening here, and I'll take the other one and keep you informed about the wisest way to pray for us. That way we can both be knowledgeable about what is happening."

"Well, let's get organized," Silvester yelled. "Everyone who is going, come over here and join me, and those who are staying behind should go over to join the Roberts."

At that time there was quite a stirring as the children and elderly went to join the prayer team, and the teens and young adults formed search parties. With that, they all set out for the mountain, with Silvester and the man who had seen the black-winged Hoover-craft in the lead.

Dr Robert's wife spoke up at that point. "Go with God's strength, and know that our prayers are going with you. May "the peace of God which transcends all understanding guard your hearts and your minds in Christ Jesus." (Phil. 4:7)

As Spite's anger against Marduk reached its climax, he screamed violently, flashed his demonic eyes at Marduk, and yelled, "Well, if you're so enthused about this Savior of yours, let Him save you from THIS!" And with that, he pulled the trigger on his Multiple Firing Laser Pistol. Immediately, Marduk's head exploded and painted a horrid picture of Spite's wrath all over the wall.

Then Spite came and got me. I had heard Spite's screaming taunts, as well as the gun exploding, so I knew that Marduk was probably dead. Fear came over me, and I began to think of what I might say to avoid the same fate for myself.

Then God spoke to me and asked me, "Would you do this for a friend?"

"I think I would do it for a friend." God continued with his questioning. "Would you allow your son to do this for an enemy?"

My first response was, "No! I would never allow my son to do this for anybody!"

Suddenly, it was as if the realization hit me like a hammer on the back of my head. Yes! God had loved me so much that He sent His own Son to come and die for me and the rest of His enemies! Of course I could stand up for Him now. Just then, I heard a key jingling in the door lock.

Spite came into my cell and pushed me roughly out into the dark hallway. "Come and see what has happened to your friend, Marduk. The same will happen to you if you do not renounce your faith in Jesus. Do you see what happened to Marduk? All the blood and crud on the wall is what remains of him and his faith."

I had been forewarned by hearing the blast as the gun fired its deathly charge, but nothing could have prepared me for what I saw all over the wall and the floor. Marduk's blood covered everything, with little splotches of brain, flesh and hair. I could see one of his eyes, staring at me from the corner of the room.

"I previously knew Marduk. Before I kill you, I'd like to know who you are. Tell me something about yourself. Where are you from? What do or did your parents do? How or when did you get involved with this Jesus guru stuff?"

"Well, my name is Victor, and my parents' names were Esther and Paul. My younger sister's name was Ruth, and my twin brother's name was Stephen."

For a good while, Spite had been feeling the hot tears forming in his eyes, but when Victor mentioned his given name, Stephen, Spite lost control of himself and burst into tears.

"Crivot!" he exclaimed. Crivot had been my nickname as a kid. It was an acronym formed out of the letters 'Victor'. I then responded, "Braino?"

"Is it really you?" We asked in unison. We looked at each other with a startled amazement. I was stunned to discover that my chief enemy had been my own brother. In a timid voice, I asked him, "Hey. Now that you realize that we are brothers, would you consider turning me loose?"

With a kind of sheepish shrug, Spite pulled out his laser knife, and cut my bonds. We kind of stammered awkwardly for a few minutes. Spite did not know what to say. The circumstances in each of our early lives had been the same. We had simply chosen different ways of responding to those same circumstances.

I had lived up to my name, responding victoriously, accepting the circumstances, and also relying on the strength that God offers us to help us through any difficulties.

Stephen, on the other hand, had responded in anger and resentment. He had developed hatred for God, and for anybody who bares His name. That hatred had been eating at him from the inside out, consuming anything good or beneficial, and leaving him unable to feel love or kindness for anybody.

Sensing that Spite was at the end of his rope and feeling the leading of the Holy Spirit, I reached over and touched him. "Stephen," I asked quietly, "are you feeling fulfilled just living for hatred and revenge? Do you ever feel at peace with yourself or with others? Even more than that, do you ever feel at peace with God?"

"Now that you ask me, Victor, I guess my answer would have to be 'No.' Revenge is an endless cycle; if I seek revenge on someone, they do the same to me, and it goes on, and on, and on. Each time, the payment is more severe."

"Ah, that is where God is different than us," I replied. "We disobeyed Him, deserving death. But ironically, God sent His Own Son, Jesus to die in our place!

"Imagine that! We had done nothing deserving of it; we were disobedient brats! But God loved us anyway, despite of what we were. He still loves us; He still loves you. He wants to have a personal relationship with you. He wants to be your Heavenly Father!"

"I'm sure He's just waiting to have a murderer as His son!" Spite replied sarcastically.

"Actually there is a verse in the Bible that says that God's strength is made perfect in our weaknesses. When God turns someone like Marduk into an evangelist, then that shows His transforming power."

"Hey! That's true. He changed Marduk; do you think that He can change me, too?"

"You'd better believe it! Just pray, and tell Him that you are sorry for your sins, all the bad things you've done. Thank Him for sending His Son, Jesus Christ, to earth to die for your sins, and accept the new life that He has for you!"

With that, I sat down with my brother and the two of us bowed our heads together and prayed, asking for Christ's forgiveness and for the new life that He promised.

Just then, the door flew open. Silvester and the young man named Peter ran into the room and Silvester shouted into his walky-talky, "We've found them. Victor's fine; I think that Marduk is dead, but praise God, it looks like Spite is entering new life in Christ!"

As soon as Spite had become a Follower, he began to change. First, he no longer wanted to be referred to as "Spite" and he no longer wanted to be known for his hatred of others, but desired instead to have his Savior mirrored in his life. Instead he wanted to go by his given name, "Stephen."

Secondly, he put away his old way of acting and reacting that he had used since he was very young, and he became a man of God. Daily, he would pray that God would demonstrate the fruit of the Holy Spirit in his life.

God has a wonderful way of doing the impossible in peoples' lives if they will only allow Him to. In just the same way as God had turned Saul into the missionary Paul, who led many to Christ, and had turned Marduk into an evangelist, God changed Stephen into a very effective messenger for Christ. In many ways he replaced Marduk.

As the years went by, in the face of a great amount of opposition to the gospel, especially from the government, the number of those who put their faith in Christ increased significantly. Dr. and Mrs. Roberts lived full and productive lives. When God took them home they were rejoicing in him.

Dr. Malerie and Silvester had two more children, and together, the Watts family went to serve the Lord as missionaries in South Africa.

Some of the believers died very bravely, suffering martyr's deaths, and the remainder are still serving the Lord here in Chicago.

With the Black Widows almost entirely out of commission, we Followers jumped at the opportunity to use our newly acquired liberty for the glory of God our Father.

We quickly left the confines of the drainage system during the day to share with the confused Chicagoans about our faith in Jesus. Each evening, however, we retreated to the safety of the God-provided hiding place, where we could rest securely, knowing that God Himself was our protector.

My brother Stephen and I are now well up in years, and the two of us have become best of friends. It has been very rewarding to see how God has chosen to use us in spite of our frailties.

I wrote these things down to show you that God works the best for those who love Him. Although at times the circumstances may seem very grim, God is bigger than our problems, and He can use the impossible!

Quoting something that Marduk used to say, "I've been given a second chance at life. This time, I'm living it for God!"

About the Authors

Dave Bray

Dave Bray lives at Jesus People, USA, in Chicago, Illinois. Born in Salina, Kansas, Dave moved to Illinois in 1993 with his parents. His father was a professor at North Park University and Seminary. Dave volunteers at "Belly Acres Designs," a T-shirt design company that is sponsored by Jesus People. His interest is science fiction in general and Star Wars and Star Trek in particular. He enjoys drawing and in sharing his faith through writing.

Thomas Fulghum

Tom grew up in Quito, Ecuador, where his parents served as missionaries at the Christian short wave radio station HCJB. He also lives at Jesus People, USA, where he volunteers as a "friend of seniors" for senior citizens who live in the Friendly Towers Retirement Residence, an organization that is also run by JPUSA members. He enjoys music, collecting foreign stamps, and spending time with people. The Great Commission, the sharing of his faith, is his chief concern.

www.ingramcontent.com/pod-product-compliance
Lightning Source LLC
Chambersburg PA
CBHW070042030726
47506CB00003B/827